HOME FOR
CHRISTMAS

HOME FOR CHRISTMAS

*A.S. Byatt, Lennie James
and Michael Morpurgo*

In support of The Passage

Daunt Books

This edition first published in
Great Britain in 2018 by
Daunt Books
83 Marylebone High Street
London W1U 4QW

1

A CIP catalogue record for this title
is available from the British Library.

ISBN 978-1-911547-43-3

Typeset by Marsha Swan

With thanks to TJ International for their contribution
to the printing and binding of this book

www.dauntbookspublishing.co.uk

Contents

FOREWORD

For most of us, a carol service is an essential part of Christmas. It doesn't matter where it's held. At home, in a school hall, in a local church or in a grand cathedral, the familiar words and music provide a sense of comfort, casting a warm glow across this important time of year. Familiarity and religion are natural bedfellows. The language and tunes we know by heart reinforce our belief. They are symbols of its permanence.

The same cannot be said of the secular readings that these days are included in our

Christmas celebrations. Last year, as I stood in the kitchen rehearsing my umpteenth rendition of John Betjeman's poem 'Christmas' for a carol service at which I was reading, my husband interrupted. 'Why are these readings nearly always the same poems and passages?' he asked. 'You'd think they could find some new pieces for Christmas.' And, being the sort of man he is, added: 'I think we should try.'

And so the idea was born. We decided to see if we could find some modern British authors prepared to write new words suitable for a carol service. Betjeman's poem, like Dylan Thomas's 'A Child's Christmas in Wales' or T.S. Eliot's sombre and profound 'Journey of the Magi' are festive stalwarts. But their regularity on the Christmas carol circuit rather undermines their strengths. No author, however great, can withstand endless repetition. The scriptures are the permanent spine of Christmas. Secular readings are different: they can begin to sound stale when they are included out of habit. We were looking for something that would refresh the language of our celebrations.

The Passage, the charity for the homeless in Westminster, was a natural home for the project. It holds a beautiful candlelit service every year in St Margaret's Church, Westminster Abbey. Its work in trying to relieve one of modern urban life's greatest problems was something we thought would attract the authors we hoped to involve.

Approaching authors to write something new, however short, for charity and to a Christmas deadline, is asking for a very big favour. Nevertheless we struck gold. The three who agreed to write for us not only represented an extraordinary range of talent – from famous actor and screenwriter to children's laureate to Booker Prize winner – but they also produced three pieces that flowed perfectly one into the other; three moving stories that looked at Christmas through the eyes of three different generations, childhood, parenthood and old age.

Lennie James chose childhood. He is famous the world over for his role as Morgan Jones in the television series *The Walking Dead* but he's also a playwright and screenwriter. His most recent work for the small screen, *Save Me*, tells the story of a down-and-out man living hand-to-mouth in South London who goes in search of the daughter he fathered some years earlier. Lennie, who spent eight years in care after his mother died when he was ten years old, has a deep understanding of homelessness and loss. The story he wrote is highly personal and very touching.

Dame Antonia Byatt – better known, perhaps, as A.S. Byatt – has written about parenthood. She offered us a little-known story that could not have been more perfect for our purpose. We leapt at the chance. A.S. Byatt won the Booker Prize for *Possession* in 1990 and was once named by *The Times* as one of the fifty greatest British writers since 1945. Her delicate tale about the endless love of parents for a wayward child is perfect for this trio of Christmas writings.

Sir Michael Morpurgo's every book seems to end up on the bestseller lists. His stories for children are loved all over the world and his book, *War Horse*, was made into a film that was nominated for just about every award there is. Since 1976 he and his wife, Clare, have run a charity that allows city children to enjoy and appreciate life in the countryside. His charming story rounds off our threesome as an elderly woman remembers Christmases past. Michael Morpurgo chose to read it himself at The Passage carol service.

The stories in this book all turned out to be about Christmas at home but three very different homes. And they were created for the benefit of those who are home*less*. Written out of charity *for* charity by three of Britain's finest authors, they form a collection that makes a unique contribution to our enjoyment of the season. In them you will find hope mixed with loss and sadness — emotions that all of us may feel at some point during the festivities. They were heard first at a carol service in central London in mid-December 2018. We hope they will be heard again by congregations at carol services in years to come. Christmas cannot always be happy but it should always be generous. These stories, a gift to our national celebrations, are a reflection of that generosity.

Sue Lawley
Christmas 2018

HOME FOR
CHRISTMAS

THE HOPES AND FEARS OF ALL THE YEARS

Michael Morpurgo

*T*hey should be here any minute. I have everything ready, just as I always do on Christmas Eve, just as it should be. My mulled cider is perfect, though I say it myself, one of my best. Harry will love it. But he'll come down when they're all gone. He never likes a crowd anyway. And he never liked Kitty and the other singers that much, which is a shame.

I like people to be friends, especially at Christmas. We should be friends at Christmas, don't you think? After all, even the Germans and the Tommies met in the middle and made friends – that was on Christmas Day 1914, four years before I was born. See? I've got a good memory still. Legs don't work like they used to, but who needs legs? My wheelchair is my Ferrari. I love my Ferrari.

Hear that? They've come. The carol singers have come. They're singing outside. My favourite. They always sing it. 'O Little Town of Bethlehem'. And they're singing the right tune too. One year they didn't and I told Kitty, and she put it right the next year. Dear Kitty.

I switch on the outside light for them, and open the door. They're all there, torches in hand, singing out, their voices trembling with cold. I wave them in, and in they come, Kitty first, all of them still singing as they fill the sitting room. 'The hopes and fears of all the years are met in thee tonight'.

Kitty, Mary, Joan, May, Carol, Rosemary, Gladys, Hettie, Anne, and Jim who growls rather than sings. But that's fine. He's much better at drinking my mulled cider. They scoff down their mince pies, shop-bought because I could never make pastry. And Kitty tells everyone again how old I am, a hundred this year. And they all clap and laugh and wish me a happy Christmas. Kitty bends down and kisses me. I do love Kitty, like sisters we are. Then they are gone.

It's strange when I come back into the room, because the mulled cider is still there, the jug full. The mince pies are all there, the plates piled neatly, the paper napkins on top, unused. I listen, and no one is singing carols outside the house next door.

Silly old thing you are.

Kitty's gone, they're all gone, Harry too. Don't you remember? One by one they went. Maybe I'm gone too. I hope not. Do we know it when we're gone, I wonder? I like Christmas, the carol singing especially. I won't be alone tomorrow. They'll all be with me. Kitty will help with the Brussels sprouts, Harry will grumble on.

The hopes and fears will still be there. I'll still be here to wish myself a happy Christmas. I'll have my friends with me. I'll be fine.

UNTO US A BOY IS BORN

A.S. Byatt

*T*hey went to the carol service in the village church. The church was decorated with evergreen boughs and candles glittered. The roof was dark. The vicar read the lesson. 'Unto us a boy is born. Unto us a son is given . . .' Martina's eyes brimmed with tears and her lips were tight. Her hand found Mark's, and they gripped. Then they sang the joyful songs with the others, and walked out into the dark. 'It will snow,' people were saying. 'There's a snowstorm forecast. Kent always gets it worst.'

They walked home, through the village, along the main road between bare hedges, turning into their own path which ran through oak woods and uphill to the farmhouse to which they had retired – early, both of them, they were only sixty. They kept a few sheep in a few fields, they walked, they gardened. The earth was frozen, the furrows rigid.

They had a holly wreath, shining dark, on the front door. Pinned to it was a letter in an envelope. Mark took it down. He tore it into neat shreds and put it in the basket in the hall. The dogs rushed out, sterns waving, bodies twisting with joy, eyes shining. Martina bent down and hugged them. They were a golden labrador called Baggins – slightly overweight and placid, and a liver-and-white collie called Silas, who was tricksy and swift. They had smiling faces and were loved.

'Perhaps we should give up putting the letter out,' said Mark. 'It's ten years, this time. It's not reasonable.'

'It's not reasonable to stop either. Don't you think we'd know if . . .'

The letter said, 'Dear Jonny, don't go away, wait. We have gone to the carol service in the church. Don't go away.'

They put out a different letter every time they went anywhere. It had worked in the past.

Jonny was their son, their only child. He was born in 1972, a peaceful baby, a very clever infant, a good student, gifted at maths, who had in due course gone to university in London and taken his degree. He was a big gentle young man, with a mass of hay-coloured hair and a vague look. It was only after the degree that things went wrong. He couldn't settle to any kind of work. He went off on long – and dangerous – walking holidays in the Alps or the Pyrenees, sometimes with friends, sometimes alone. He didn't give a date for his returns and was sometimes away for months. Then he went to India. 'I have to find myself,' he told them gently, and they gave him money and asked him, as urgently as they dared, to keep in touch. He didn't. They searched, they reported his loss, and he was not found. Then, one day, he simply walked back into their house, covered in bruises and skeletally thin. He stayed for a year or so, employed as a research assistant at the university, and then was off again, this time for two years. Martina had heard of other missing persons who had returned aggressive, drugged, unrecognisable. Jonny was simply milder and milder and less and less attached to the earth. They took to putting up the messages, and one of them, once, was read and they found Jonny walking to meet them when they came back from a dinner party.

But now it was ten years. They could not grieve, and increasingly could not hope, though he was on Missing Persons registers worldwide. There was a point at which the tension caused them to grow apart, into two grim silences. It was Mark who said they must stop that, and bought the dogs. The dogs were not substitute children, they were dogs. They were living creatures with needs and excitements of their own, and this was good.

It was not easy to be happy at Christmas. They got through it, cautiously. They did have a tree – a small real tree – on the top of which they always put an angel Jonny had made in primary school out of circles and triangles of creamy paper, spangled with glitter. Its head was a bit bowed after the years, but it had survived.

On Christmas day they went out for a brisk walk with the dogs. It had snowed in the night and more was forecast. The trees were spattered with cold white and the earth shone bleakly. They didn't talk much, and when they did it was about the liveliness of the dogs. Silas had his nose to the ground and suddenly found a trail, squeezed round an open gate and raced across a field to a wooden hut that stood by the further hedge. Mark called to him to come back, but he barked more and more wildly and Baggins loped after him, and joined the barking. Mark and Martina followed. Some-one had left both gate and hut door open. The barking pealed out.

Mark bent down and went in. There was a heap of straw in one corner, and, he saw, dark wet stains on the floor, which the dogs investigated. Something had killed something. In the midst of the hay was something very bright – something shiny and rose-pink, which resolved itself into one of those puffer jackets everyone wore. That too had what looked like blood-stains on it. He did not like what he thought he was going to find but nevertheless went on, and lifted the edge of the jacket. Inside it was a fuchsia fringed pashmina, also bloodstained. There was an infinitesimal breath of a sound. Inside the pashmina was a naked baby, a boy, trailing his umbilical cord and breathing – yes breathing – lightly and unevenly.

Martina came, and saw him. She had been a maternity nurse and knew what to do. She cleared his nose and mouth, saw to his cord as best she could, swaddled him tightly in the pashmina, and put him inside her fleecy jacket, his face against her own skin. He made another mewing sound. The dogs leapt and celebrated.

They hurried home, under a darkening, steely sky, the cold biting, the coming snow heavy in the air. They took down the message in the wreath. Martina went into a flurry of activity, tearing up towels and blankets, making a cup of boiled sugary water, holding the warming boy against her own warmth, weeping briefly. Mark said they must ring the emergency services.

Martina said, 'Where can the mother be? She can't be far or he would have been dead by now.'

'There weren't tracks. It must have snowed after she left. I'd best go out and search. She must be in a bad way.'

By now it was snowing very heavily. Fat grey clouds hung close and poured out more and more.

Mark went out with the dogs. Martina sat in the rocking chair by the fire, with the small creature close against her skin and sang to him. What came into her mind was,

'In the bleak midwinter
Frosty wind made moan
Earth stood hard as iron
Water like a stone.'

He gave a little snort, and drifted into sleep. She held him.

Mark gave the dogs the puffer jacket to sniff and set out down the hill, with the snow driving into his face. The dogs rushed on, indefatigable, back towards the hut and then on their usual walk, which crossed the fields towards Frog Pond. Frog Pond was on a public right of way and was signed. Mark thought that perhaps the dogs were letting him down and just going to where they liked to play. But when they came near the pond they set up their triumphant chorus again, Silas twisted and made little rushes, Baggins walked to the edge of the water, where someone very still was lying under a blanket of snow, her face on the frozen surface of the water. There was a halo of white-blonde hair on the ice and a slate-blue outstretched hand.

She was not dead, but was deeply unconscious. She was small and frail and looked like a schoolgirl – maybe was a schoolgirl – with a sharp bony face, and a kind of shapeless sack-dress over twisted black leggings. Mark picked her up, shook off the snow, stuffed her arms into the puffer jacket and slung her over his shoulder. It was a good thing he was fit. The wind was against him, and the snow filled his eyes and annihilated his sight of the vanishing tracks. Baggins and Silas rushed ahead and came back for him, rushed ahead and came back, and he followed them, and so came home, into the warmth, and shook off the snow on the girl and himself.

Then he took the infant – 'put him against your skin' said Martina – whilst she saw to the girl, wrapping her in a warm nightdress and a blanket, cleaning away the blood. 'She needs stitches,' said Martina – making warm chicken broth.

'We should get the emergency services,' said Mark.

'Can they get out here?' said Martina. 'The lane's frozen, there'll be black ice on the main road.'

They telephoned. The emergency services were in trouble on the roads where the snow had caused blockages and pile-ups in the traffic. They did not think they could get through. They would look into helicopters but visibility was terrible. Mark said that his wife was a maternity nurse and she was looking after mother and child, but there were supplies she really needed.

The girl stirred, in the end, and opened her eyes. She was cocooned in sheets and blankets on the sofa by the fire. She stared and shivered. Martina could see her thinking. The girl said, in a whisper of a voice, 'I meant to be dead. I tried.'

Martina gave her some soup. She stared for a moment and then drank. She turned her face away.

'I've done something horrible. I meant to be dead.'

Martina said, 'It's all right. We found him. You wrapped him up well. I saw to him. I'm a nurse. My husband and the dogs found you. You're all right here. Is there anyone we should get in touch with?'

'No one. I've got no one.'

Martina sat and talked gently. Her name, the girl said, was Emmy. Everything had gone terribly wrong. Pressed about parents – or maybe a boyfriend – she said she had run away from home when she found she was pregnant – 'they'd never forgive me, I have done something

terrible to them – '. She said she and her boyfriend had been living in a squat in Brighton
– 'nicking things, you know, people came and
went, no questions asked – '. She spoke Estu-
ary English, could have come from anywhere.
'Then they all got scared when they saw how
big I was, they said I'd got to go home – Jerry
– my boyfriend – was more interested in Pixie
by then, I could tell, I wasn't much fun for
him . . .'

The baby began to cry. More strongly than
before, more unhappily.

'He's hungry. Do you want to see him?'

'No,' said Emmy wildly. 'No I don't. He was
a mistake, I'm no good to him . . .'

'You wrapped him up well. He needs feed-
ing. We can't get out to get formula. Only you
can feed him.' Martina was steely as well as
gentle.

'No, no I can't,' said Emmy, but Martina
fetched the baby, with his washed blond-white
hair and his delicate little face, and laid him

beside his mother. He opened his eyes, and waved a small hand weakly. His lips moved.

'Oh—' said Emmy. 'He was such a mess, I thought something awful was wrong with him. Look at his face.' She began to cry. 'Look at his face.'

'I was a maternity nurse. You are in the right place. I can show you exactly what to do.'

Emmy said 'No' again, more doubtfully, but did not resist when Martina put the baby to her breast, only gave a little cry of surprise which might have been either happy or unhappy. The baby knew what to do. After a moment Emmy adjusted her arms to make him more comfortable and then clutched him to her.

Martina said, 'Where were you going? How did you come here?'

'They said I had to go home. They put me on the bus to . . . I didn't think I could go home, I think my mother would have pushed me out when she saw me – but I thought when I got off the bus I'd go to the hospital in – and ask them to help me. And then all the pain began so I got off the bus when it stopped and just walked – I thought I'd kill myself, drown myself, there was a notice to a pond – and then he got born – and I didn't want to drown him – I was all confused . . .'

'I think I should try to speak to your mother. She must miss you very much.'

'She won't forgive me.'

'Will you let me ask her?'

The voice at the other end of the line was light and anxious and made distant by crackling and hissing noises. Martina suddenly and belatedly wondered if she would know how to say the right thing.

'Mrs Andrews?'

'Who is that?'

'Do you have a daughter called Emmy?'

'I did. But I think she's dead.'

'No, she isn't. She's here, safe, in my house. She said I might phone you.'

There was a very long silence.

'She's had a bad time. She's confused. She thinks you will be angry with her.'

The other woman was weeping along the wires, trying to stop weeping and speak. Martina took a chance.

'Mrs Andrews. There's a baby. A boy. Born this morning. Mrs Andrews?'

'I did wonder,' said the other voice. 'Of course you wonder.'

'She thought you would be angry – tell her to go away – '

A long pause. Then, 'I am angry. I'm angry she didn't trust me. Is that boy there – Jerry? I'm angry at all this time – searching and wondering – '

'No. He isn't here.'

'Can I come to see her?'

'We're snowed in. The emergency services

can't get here even. Fortunately I was a sister on a maternity ward.'

'Can I speak to her?'

'I'll ask her. She's very weak. She was lying in the snow.'

'I will thank you properly when . . .'

Martina carried the phone to Emmy, and took the baby and held him whilst Emmy spoke to her mother, though as far as Martina could hear two people were crying into two phones and occasionally saying, 'It's all right.' She looked at the baby and his vague gaze rested on her. She held him close and kissed him. 'I hope you have more sense than your mother,' she told him quietly, and he snuffled and snuggled.

In the late afternoon a helicopter thrummed above the garden. Baggins and Silas barked as though England was being invaded. The phone rang. Mark answered. It was the emergency services who said they were dropping a packet of things until they could get through. Mark reported that mother and child were doing well and Martina was in charge. The packages fell through the grey air, the dogs rushed out and stood by, Martin gathered them up.

They had antibiotics, milk and nappies. They had pretty little towelling suits, and cardigans and various medicines that might be needed, just in case. There were also mince pies, a Christmas pudding, some chocolate and two cards – one wishing everyone a very happy Christmas, and one for the new baby and his mother with good wishes for the future.

Martina warmed up the mince pies and opened a bottle of champagne. They sat round the blazing fire, and dozed, and chatted, and centred their attention on the baby, which is what always happens.

Martina sat next to the plain little tree with its bent-headed angel. She nodded at it. She said to Mark, 'We used to have fairy-lights. I'll seek them out.'

THAT FIRST
WITHOUT HER
CHRISTMAS DAY

Lennie James

*M*y memory remembers snow. A white carpet over Tooting Bec common, from North Drive to Emmanuel Road; a black-sludge track made by cars heading to and from the South Circular the only break in the brilliance. Kids skating on what was left and frozen in the Lido, and a perfect yellow round in the sea-blue sky, peeking over a Grade II listed mansion with a roof of crystal flakes.

Inside that mansion . . . inside that home . . . inside that kids' home, our home . . . we were eighteen. Eighteen kids billeted in council care. Our real homes snapped, cracked or broken. It was the year Elvis died. It was the day that Captain Mainwaring would call Elton John a 'stupid boy' on Eric and Ern's Christmas Special. It was three months before that day that we lost our mum. I had known her for ten years, my brother for twelve, and then no more.

It was the first of five Christmases we would spend in that eleven-bedroomed Georgian house with its garden the size of a football pitch and with those sixteen others unrelated. Most of them still had parents, just ones, for one reason or other, incapable.

I waited for my brother to make a noise like he was awake before I made a noise like I was. I think we were each waiting for the other, so who knows how long we had lain there, trying to be brave enough to start this First Without Her Christmas Day. He led the way. He knew he had to. He knew I couldn't. I had all but stopped talking in the three months since.

I'd have stayed in bed if he hadn't done what he thought big brothers should do and led the way.

The Christmas table ran the length of this double room, with its oak panelled walls and elaborately corniced ceiling. The table was laid for eighteen, plus Michelle's mum and the staff working on that First Without Her Christmas Day – Aunties Nicky and Christine with Michael and Kathy.

We were all allowed to come down in our dressing gowns or PJs. The others collected hugs and 'Merry Christmases' from each other and staff, both those working and those who came in just for the morning. My big brother pulled me to his side. I don't know if it was for my benefit or his. There was a circle of chairs around the outside of the room each with a name on it and a plastic shopping bag brimming with wrapped presents by its side. Aunty Nicky said, 'Find your name. Find your chair.' I was certain there'd been a mistake.

Paul, who was my age but London Irish, had already told us that the council only offered five quid per kid for prezzies, so the bounty in the bags made no sense at all. Aunty Nicky said, 'Merry Christmas and get going!' and the other sixteen tore at the wrapping paper to get to the presents inside. We didn't. Us two. No one there really knew us. Who'd be giving us all that was in those bags? Our mum loved Christmas. She saved all year for it. Except for when Muhammad Ali was on TV, Christmas was the biggest party in our flat and she'd be the life and soul – in our flat, on our road and at our church. We wouldn't get much, but there'd always be one thing unexpected, beyond wished for, that'd make us go, 'Wow!'

Aunty Nicky assured us that we really could unwrap what was by our names. My big brother went first and I followed. My memory doesn't remember all I unwrapped. There were two annuals – one Spiderman, one Planet of the Apes, a Jackson Five cassette, bike lights, a scarf, a hat, a tracksuit and now I'm just guess-remembering like I'm on *The Generation Game*. There was much more than you'd ever get from five pounds, that's for sure. And that wasn't the end of it. After turkey and before Xmas pud we each received our 'main' present at the dinner table. Mine was a Newporter Sprint skateboard – blue deck and red wheels. It was exactly what I wanted and beyond what I could have hoped for. I screamed, 'Wow!'

That First Without Her Christmas Day is one I have never forgotten. Not for how it started, the dread of being without our mother's life and soul, but for the kindness, care, consideration and generosity shown to we two of eighteen by people unknown and unrelated to us. A terrible thing had happened to us just three months before. But we got lucky. We eighteen were in care and we were being cared for. Swelling the council's meagre Christmas allowance with their own money was just one example of how.

Knowing that a blue-and-red skateboard would help a kid, all but silenced by his grief, to giggle like it was Christmas Day was another. I've never found out how they knew, but I think it had something to do with what big brothers do for little brothers.

ABOUT
THE PASSAGE

Founded in 1980, The Passage is a charity working to end street homelessness. Its work is based on the principles of St Vincent de Paul, a Christian social reformer of the early seventeenth century who believed that vulnerable people needed to be helped by action, not words. Today the charity's services are in higher demand than ever before.

All kinds of people can become homeless: redundancy, home repossession, a broken marriage, mental illness, violence or abuse can all result in men and women losing the roofs over their heads. Westminster has the highest incidence of rough sleeping in the UK. Over the years, in addition to providing accommodation and homelessness prevention services, The Passage has established the country's largest resource centre for homeless people, helping and taking care of 150 men and women on a daily basis.

Its aim is to provide them with the resources they need to transform their own lives. It not only offers shelter, hot food, showers, clothing and medical care, but also gives advice and helps people into work, into accommodation, and importantly, reunites them with their families from whom they have come adrift.

Since its foundation, the charity has helped more than 120,000 people to end their homelessness. All this has been achieved through love and care. As St Vincent de Paul said, 'Judge persons and things in the most favourable light, at all times and under all circumstances.'

The Passage would like to extend sincere thanks to Sue Lawley and Hugh Williams for their idea of inviting authors to write new pieces for Christmas and their efforts in bringing it to fruition. It would like to thank everyone at St Margaret's Church, Westminster Abbey for permitting The Passage to use their lovely church each year for the charity's carol service. The Passage would also like to thank A.S. Byatt, Lennie James and Michael Morpurgo for their personal and creative contributions that make up the body of this work. Finally, it wishes to extend gratitude to Daunt Books for the publication of this booklet and their most generous support of the charity's work. All proceeds from the sale of the book will be donated to The Passage.

For more information about The Passage,
or to make a donation or
offer practical help, please visit

www.passage.org.uk

or call 020 7592 1850